BABY DUCKLING

Written by Sarah Toast
Illustrated by Judith Love

7373 North Cicero Avenue
Lincolnwood, Illinois 60712

Ground Floor, 59 Gloucester Place
London W1U 8JJ

Permission is never granted for commercial purposes.

Customer Service: 1-800-595-8484 or customer_service@pilbooks.com

www.pilbooks.com

p i kids is a registered trademark of Publications International, Ltd.

8 7 6 5 4 3 2 1

Manufactured in China.

ISBN-10: 1-4127-9901-5
ISBN-13: 978-1-4127-9901-0

publications international, ltd.

It is summer, and Mother Duck is making a nest. In a clump of reeds near the edge of the pond, Mother Duck finds a hollow place in the ground. She lines it with grass and soft cattail stems.

Mother Duck lays her nine smooth eggs. She plucks soft feathers from her breast to line the nest.

 **FUN FACT**

A tiny duck is growing inside each egg. It is attached to a bag of thick yellow liquid called yolk. Yolk is special food for the growing baby duck.

Mother Duck sits on her nine eggs for many days and nights. Whenever she leaves the nest, she covers her eggs with a soft blanket of down to hide them and keep them warm.

At last Mother Duck hears the "pip-pip" of her ducklings working to get out of their shells. The last little duckling to break out of its shell is Dabble.

? How do ducklings break out of their shells?
Baby ducklings peck their way out by using a special egg tooth. Located on the tip of the beak, this egg tooth will fall off later.

Mother Duck protects her little ducklings by rubbing her tummy feathers over them in the nest. Now the ducklings are waterproof. They will stay warm and dry when they swim.

Mother Duck can waterproof her own feathers by combing oil into them with her bill. The oil that she uses comes from a place near her tail.

FUN FACT

When ducks rub oil over their feathers, it is called preening.

While the ducklings are resting in their nest, a skunk comes to the water's edge for a drink. Mother Duck and the ducklings try to stay perfectly still and quiet so the skunk will not notice them.

Mother Duck's spotted brown feathers and the stripes on her ducklings blend in with the tall grasses and reeds.

 **FUN FACT**
Ducklings stay very close to their mother for about two months, or until they can fly.

Dabble is a special type of duck known as a dabbling duck. She sees Mother Duck taking care of her brothers and sisters. She knows that her mother will take good care of her, too.

The tiny ducklings are less than a day old, but they can run. They follow their mother down to the water's edge for their very first swim.

 **FUN FACT**
The mother duck must waterproof her ducklings' feathers before she takes them for their first swim.

Dabble is the first young duckling to jump into the water after Mother Duck. Her sisters and brothers gleefully jump in after her. They bob on the water like little balls of fluff.

What a glorious and fun pond! Dabble is dazzled by a dragonfly that lands on a nearby lily pad. She stares at a caterpillar on a cattail leaf.

What do ducks eat in the winter?
In the winter, it is more difficult to find insects, seeds, or plants to eat. So every fall, some ducks fly south in a V formation. The weather is warm there, and they will find plenty of food.

Now Dabble is getting quite hungry, and she knows exactly what to do. She tips up her tail and stretches her bill down to the muddy bottom of the pond to find plenty of plants, roots, and seeds.

Dabble enjoys dipping down to look for food underwater, then popping up again to find Mother Duck.

?

What does dabbling mean?

Dabbling is what Dabble does when she turns upside down to look for food underwater. Only her tail can be seen above the water.

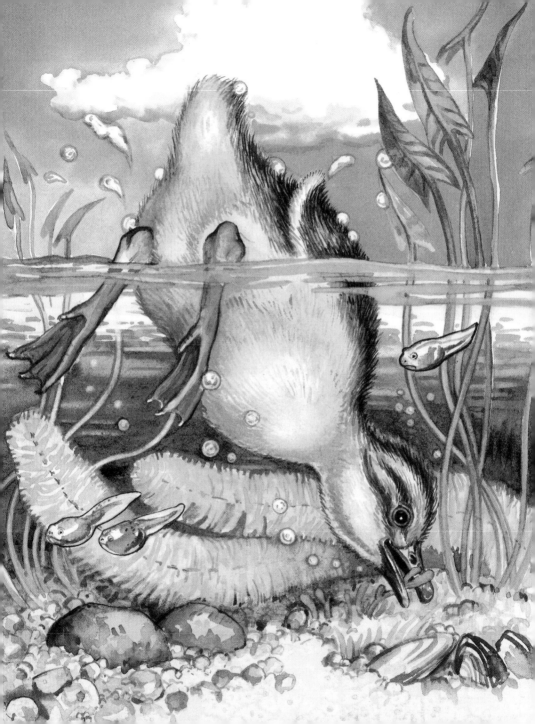

Dabble watches a colorful butterfly flitting among the reeds in the pond. Then Dabble dips down to enjoy another nibble. She lifts her tiny head to quack hello to a red-winged blackbird.

Mother Duck dips down into the water to get something to eat, too. Underwater, Mother Duck sees a big snapping turtle swimming toward her little ducklings.

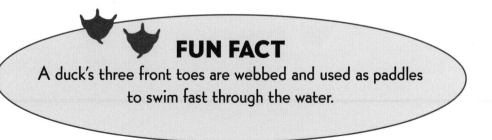

FUN FACT

A duck's three front toes are webbed and used as paddles to swim fast through the water.

Just as quick as a quack, Mother Duck calls out to her ducklings to return to shore, but Dabble is underwater and doesn't hear her.

Mother Duck swims swiftly over to Dabble and gets between Dabble and the snapping turtle. Dabble pops up and swims to shore with Mother Duck, and the turtle swims away.

FUN FACT

A mother duck will do anything to protect her ducklings. Sometimes she will flap her wings and quack loudly to scare an enemy away.

That night all the ducklings sleep, warm and safe in the nest after their busy first day in the world. Dabble is dreaming of tomorrow, when she will see the bright butterfly again.